The wonderful thing about Michael Rosen's words for
We're Going on a Bear Hunt is the space they leave for an
illustrator to imagine. The reader is never told who 'we' are
and so it was left entirely open to me how to imagine the
characters. The scenes with the snowstorm and the mud
are also never described, and so again it was up to me
to decide how they looked. All this openness presented me
with a chance to revisit the Suffolk landscapes of my own
childhood and to remember the joy of exploring the fields
and beaches with my older brother, John.
It was also a chance to consider the tenderness of our
bear's feelings as he returns, alone, to his dark cave.
What I could never, ever have imagined, though, as I sat in my
studio all those years ago, painting the family of brothers and
sisters and their collie dog splish-splashing, squelch-squerching
and stumble-tripping, was that 30 years on children all over
the world would continue joining in on our Bear Hunt.

Helen Oxenbury.

For Geraldine, Joe, Naomi,
Eddie, Laura and Isaac
M.R.

For Amelia
H.O.

First published 1989 by Walker Books Ltd
87 Vauxhall Walk, London SE11 5HJ

This edition published 2019

10 9 8 7 6 5 4 3 2 1

Text © 1989 Michael Rosen
Illustrations © 1989 Helen Oxenbury
Additional text © 2019 Helen Oxenbury

The right of Michael Rosen and Helen Oxenbury
to be identified as author and illustrator respectively
of this work has been asserted by them in accordance
with the Copyright, Designs and Patents Act 1988

This book has been typeset in Veronan Light Educational

Printed in China

British Library Cataloguing in Publication Data:
a catalogue record for this book is available from
the British Library

ISBN: 978-1-4063-8677-6

www.walker.co.uk
www.jointhebearhunt.com

We're Going on a Bear Hunt

30TH ANNIVERSARY EDITION

Retold by
Michael Rosen

Illustrated by
Helen Oxenbury

WALKER BOOKS
AND SUBSIDIARIES
LONDON • BOSTON • SYDNEY • AUCKLAND

We're going on a bear hunt.

We're going to catch a big one.

What a beautiful day!

We're not scared.

Uh-uh! Grass!

Long wavy grass.

We can't go over it.

We can't go under it.

Oh no!

We've got to go through it!

Swishy swashy!
Swishy swashy!
Swishy swashy!

We're going on a bear hunt.

We're going to catch a big one.

What a beautiful day!

We're not scared.

Uh-uh! A river!
A deep cold river.
We can't go over it.
We can't go under it.

Oh no!
We've got to go through it!

Splash splosh!
Splash splosh!
Splash splosh!

We're going on a bear hunt.

We're going to catch a big one.

What a beautiful day!

We're not scared.

Uh-uh! Mud!

Thick oozy mud.

We can't go over it.

We can't go under it.

Oh no!

We've got to go through it!

Squelch squerch!
Squelch squerch!
Squelch squerch!

We're going on a bear hunt.

We're going to catch a big one.

What a beautiful day!

We're not scared.

Uh-uh! A forest!

A big dark forest.

We can't go over it.

We can't go under it.

Oh no!

We've got to go through it!

Stumble trip!
Stumble trip!
Stumble trip!

We're going on a bear hunt.

We're going to catch a big one.

What a beautiful day!

We're not scared.

Uh-uh! A snowstorm!

A swirling whirling snowstorm.

We can't go over it.

We can't go under it.

Oh no!

We've got to go through it!

Hoooo woooo!
Hoooo woooo!
Hoooo woooo!

We're going on a bear hunt.

We're going to catch a big one.

What a beautiful day!

We're not scared.

Uh-uh! A cave!

A narrow gloomy cave.

We can't go over it.

We can't go under it.

Oh no!

We've got to go through it!

Tiptoe!

     Tiptoe!

          Tiptoe!

WHAT'S THAT?

One shiny wet nose!

Two big furry ears!

Two big goggly eyes!

IT'S A BEAR!!!!

Quick! Back through the cave! Tiptoe! Tiptoe! Tiptoe!

Back through the snowstorm! Hoooo wooooo! Hoooo wooooo!

Back through the forest! Stumble trip! Stumble trip! Stumble trip!

Back through the mud! Squelch squerch! Squelch squerch!

Back through the river! Splash splosh! Splash splosh! Splash splosh!

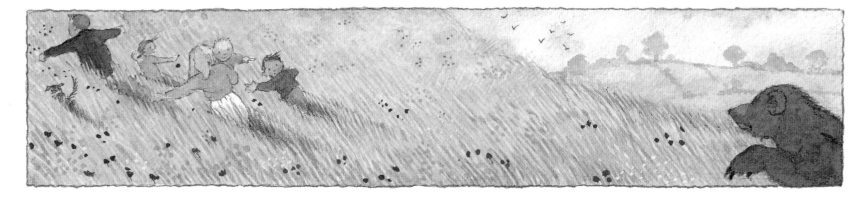

Back through the grass! Swishy swashy! Swishy swashy!

Get to our front door.

Open the door.

Up the stairs.

Oh no!

We forgot to shut the door.

Back downstairs.

Shut the door.

Back upstairs.

Into the bedroom.

Into bed.

Under the covers.

We're not going on

a bear hunt again.

Other brilliant versions of the ultimate join-in book

We're Going on a Bear Hunt
30TH ANNIVERSARY EDITION

Michael Rosen   Helen Oxenbury

ISBN 978-1-4063-8676-9 (Board book)

We're Going on a Bear Hunt
SOUND BOOK

Michael Rosen   Helen Oxenbury

PRESS THE BUTTONS AND
JOIN IN THE BEAR HUNT!

ISBN 978-1-4063-5738-7

We're Going on a Bear Hunt
A POP-UP EDITION

Michael Rosen   Helen Oxenbury

ISBN 978-1-4063-6619-8

We're Going on a Bear Hunt
STICKER ACTIVITY BOOK

WITH OVER 50 STICKERS

Michael Rosen   Helen Oxenbury

ISBN 978-1-4063-6192-6

We're Going on a Bear Hunt
COLOURING BOOK

WITH BEAR EARS TO MAKE

Michael Rosen   Helen Oxenbury

ISBN 978-1-4063-6191-9

We're Going on a Bear Hunt
ACTIVITY FUN BOOK

BAKE YOUR OWN BEAR PAW BISCUITS

Michael Rosen   Helen Oxenbury

ISBN 978-1-4063-7077-5

Available from all good booksellers

www.walker.co.uk   www.jointhebearhunt.com